GW00866053

This book belongs to:

_ _ _ _ _ _ _ _ _ _ _ _ _ _ _

_ _ _ _ _ _ _ _ _ _ _ _ _ _ _

# Nettie's New House

Lynda Britnell . Joanna Walsh

Orion
Children's Books

First published in Great Britain in 1996
by Orion Children's Books
a division of the Orion Publishing Group Ltd
Orion House
5 Upper St Martin's Lane
London WC2H 9EA

A catalogue record for this book is available from the British Library
Printed in Great Britain

Nettie Mugwort the fairy lived
in a hollow log in the forest.

All summer her friends
came to visit her there,
Know-It-All the gnome,
Bluebell the fairy,
and Mr Beechtree who owned the sweetshop.

During the day the friends would sit
and have tea and honeycakes,
and in the evening they would watch
the sun go down.

But as summer came to an end the weather got colder.
The wind blew leaves and twigs into Nettie's home.
The rain blew in and made her mats and chairs wet,
and her friends didn't like coming to visit her
because it was so cold inside the log.

One morning Bluebell came to see Nettie.
"Good morning, Nettie," said Bluebell,
but Nettie didn't answer.
She was sitting in a chair
holding a cup of tea and sniffing loudly.
"Oh Nettie, what is the matter?" asked Bluebell.
"I don't feel well," said Nettie,
rubbing her red nose.
"All night long it rained, the wind blew
and now I've got a horrible cold."

"We will have to find you a new *warm* home,"
said Bluebell. "Come along."

So Nettie and Bluebell went off
to find Nettie a new home.

some
fairy
houses

The town was full of toadstool houses.
Some were small with flat tops.
Some were middle-sized with domed tops.
Some were large with spotted tops.

Inside a fairy house

Nettie stood beside a small flat-topped toadstool.
"This is no good," said Nettie,
"I'm taller than the roof of this house."

Then Nettie and Bluebell went to see
a middle-sized toadstool with a domed roof.

"This is bigger," said Bluebell.
"Yes, it is," said Nettie,

"but I will have to crawl through the front door.
It is still not big enough."

Next they went to a large toadstool
with a high spotted roof.
"This will be big enough," said Bluebell.
Nettie could just get through the door
but when she tried to stand up straight
inside the toadstool...
*BOMP!* She hit her head on the ceiling.
"Oh dear," said Bluebell.
"We don't have any bigger toadstools.
Where are you going to live?"

The two friends walked sadly
to Mr Beechtree's sweet shop.
Bluebell told Mr Beechtree
how all the toadstools were too small.

"Have you looked at the old oak tree across the path?" said Mr Beechtree. "No one has lived there for a long time because it is too big."

Nettie, Bluebell and Mr Beechtree hurried to the old oak tree.

Mr Beechtree pushed open the door.
The doorway was much bigger than Nettie,
so she didn't have to crawl in.
And the ceiling was much higher
so Nettie didn't bang her head.
Nettie looked around and smiled.
"This will be my new home," she said.

Know-It-All, Bluebell and Mr Beechtree
all helped Nettie
carry her table and chairs,

her plates and cups and her bed
into the old oak tree.

When they had put everything
safely in her new home,
Nettie and her friends
had a lovely tea
of lemonade and honeycakes.

And Nettie Mugwort has lived
in the old oak tree ever since.